Zachary

Harold

To Tracey and Josh, two of the happiest campers I know
—A. K.

Too itchy and red
—D. C.

MARGARET K. McELDERRY BOOKS
An imprint of Simon & Schuster Children's Publishing Division
1230 Avenue of the Americas, New York, New York 10020
Text copyright © 2011 by Alan Katz
Illustrations copyright © 2011 by David Catrow
All rights reserved, including the right of reproduction in whole or in part in any form.
MARGARET K. McELDERRY BOOKS is a trademark of Simon & Schuster, Inc.
For information about special discounts for bulk purchases, please contact Simon &
Schuster Special Sales at 1–866–506–1949 or business@simonandschuster.com.
The Simon & Schuster Speakers Bureau can bring authors to your live event. For more
information or to book an event, contact the Simon & Schuster Speakers Bureau at
1–866–248–3049 or visit our website at www.simonspeakers.com.
Book edited by Emma D. Dryden
Book designed by Sonia Chaghatzbanian
The text for this book is set in Kosmik.
The illustrations for this book are rendered in watercolors, colored pencil, and ink.
Manufactured in China
0211 SCP
2 4 6 8 10 9 7 5 3 1
Library of Congress Cataloging-in-Publication Data
Katz, Alan.
Mosquitoes are ruining my summer! : and other silly dilly camp songs / Alan Katz ; illustrated
by David Catrow. — 1st ed.   p. cm.
Summary: Familiar tunes are given new words relating to summer camp, including "Whose
Idea Was This Dumb Hike" sung to the tune of "Twinkle Twinkle Little Star."
ISBN 978-1-4169-5568-9 (hardcover)
1. Children's songs, English—United States—Texts. 2. Camps—Songs and music—Texts.
[1. Camps—Songs and music. 2. Songs.] I. Catrow, David, ill. II. Title.
PZ8.3.K1275Mo 2011   782.42—dc22   2009021167

FIRST
EDITION

Mosquitoes are ruining my summer!

and other silly dilly camp songs

by **Alan Katz**

illustrated by **David Catrow**

MARGARET K. McELDERRY BOOKS
NEW YORK   LONDON   TORONTO   SYDNEY

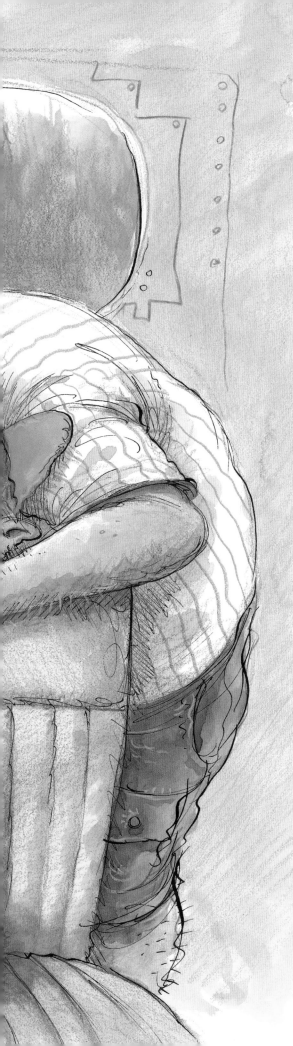

On the Bus Ride
(To the tune of "Yankee Doodle")

On the bus ride
off to camp,
alone with fifty strangers.
Kids are crying.
Seats are damp.
Ahead . . . who knows what dangers?
We stop off,
pick up ten more—
all sixty misbehaving.
Sitting with a
kid who says he's
eight . . . and yet he's shaving!

As the driver speeds it up,
kids fly in the aisles.
Don't think I can keep this up
for three hundred more miles!
Stop for lunch—
they give us each
a bowl of cold spaghetti.
No one ate;
instead they made
it meatballs and confetti!

I know I will treasure camp
and the friends I met there.
Only thing I hope and pray
is someday we will get there!

This Whole Bunk Is Very Cluttered
(To the tune of "The Battle Hymn of the Republic")

I think the camp brochure might have been lying 'bout my bunk,
'cause everywhere I look I see some wet and musty junk.
I share the room with Tony, Mickey, Larry, and . . . a skunk
(and Mickey smells the worst!).

This whole bunk is very cluttered.
One deep breath and we all sputtered.
All the walls are peanut-buttered.
There's dust beyond belief!

At night I do not need a woolen blanket on my bed,
'cause spiders in the room come by to weave me one instead.
I think I'd be more comfortable just sleeping on a sled.
It's nice, if you like filth!

This whole place is really dirty.
Let me tell you, it is dirty.
Oh boy, it is really dirty.
So dirty, I can't rhyme!

I'm gonna write my folks a letter 'bout this doom and gloom
and ask them for a superturbo-action-size vacuum.
I can't wait till it's time to go back home to my bedroom.
Compared to this . . . it's clean!

Somebody Send Me Home Now!
(To the tune of "Skip to My Lou")

Please excuse me if I am terse:
The camp meals could not be worse.
Lousy food—served by the nurse.
Somebody send a cookbook!

Skip, skip, skip every meal.
Skip, skip, skip every meal.
Skip, skip, skip every meal.
Skip every meal, I warn you!

Breakfast—it's
banana peel,
fresh cement
they call oatmeal.
Bite the sausage, you'll both squeal.
Somebody send a doctor!

Skip, skip, skip every meal.
Skip, skip, skip every meal.
Skip, skip, skip every meal.
Skip every meal, I warn you!

Lunch—a treat—
mystery goo.
Slurp it up—
no need to chew.
For dessert: devil's food shoe.
Somebody send a pizza!

Skip, skip, skip every meal.
Skip, skip, skip every meal.
Skip, skip, skip every meal.
Skip every meal, I warn you!

Dinnertime, so
grab a tray.
The main course
will probably neigh.
Meals should not
gallop away.
Somebody send me home now!

Mosquitoes Are Ruining My Summer
(To the tune of "My Bonnie Lies Over the Ocean")

Mosquitoes are ruining my summer.
Mosquitoes from morning till night.
Mosquitoes have made life a bummer,
'cause it's only me that they bite!

Itching, scratching,
I spray on repellent.
They scoff, they scoff.
More are hatching.
I just tell them all to buzz off!

Mosquitoes are planning to get me.
Mosquitoes have lunch on my arm.
Mosquitoes each day sure upset me.
They spell out my name when they swarm!

Scratching, itching,
I'm wearing long sleeves and
long pants, long pants.
Got me twitching.
(Though I did win first prize for dance!)

Mosquitoes are daily attacking.
Mosquitoes think I'm a delight.
Mosquitoes wait in line for snacking.
Soon there'll be no me left to bite!

Itching, scratching . . .
The nurse said eat garlic—
I did, I did.
No mosquitoes!
(But also no counselors or kids!)

Oh, Send Me a Package
(To the tune of "On Top of Old Smokey")

Oh, send me a package:
a package with stuff.
Don't care how gigantic,
it won't be enough.

Some kids receive candy—
that's such a nice gift.
Make sure you send something
too heavy to lift.

I could use new headphones,
top-10 DVDs,
a laptop computer,
a mountain of cheese.

Do not forget cookies,
a personal fridge,
and 'cause I like quiet
I need a drawbridge.

Don't want to cause trouble.
Hope you won't complain,
but I'd like to ask for
Montana and Maine.

Hey, throw in Nebraska.
Wow, that would be grand.
But if they're too large, just
please send Rhode Island.

The Laundry Blues
(To the tune of "The Mexican Hat Dance")

No shirts,
no suits,
no shorts,
nothing I can wear for sports.
No socks,
no briefs,
no pants,
not one thing clean for the dance!

Fresh towels? Ha!
No way.
I use the same one each day.
And as
for underwear,
don't ask what is under there!

Oh . . . four weeks and I haven't done laundry.
No soap has come close to my clothes.
I look at the pile forlornly
and choose what I'm wearing by . . . nose!

Trying Out for the Camp Show
(To the tune of "Take Me Out to the Ball Game")

Trying out for the camp show . . .
All stand back, I'm a star.
Hand me a harp and flute.
Listen, I'm
able to play them both
at the same time!
And I tap, tap, tap
like a master.
I juggle while I do flips.
Watch my act with puppets—
you won't see me move my lips!

Next up, it's time for magic:
I make things disappear.
Singing's so beautiful, you will cry.
I'll crack your glasses with notes oh so high.
Yes, I'm lo-, lo-, loaded with talent.
I'm full of stuff that excites.
What's that? Now that you've seen my act,
I should work the lights?

Arts and Crafts Time
(To the tune of "Old MacDonald Had a Farm")

Arts and crafts time:
Oh boy, clay—
this will sure be fun.
They will all yell "hip hooray"
when my vase is done.
With a pinch, pinch here
and a push, push there;
here a smack, there a whack—
looks more like a flapjack.
Arts and crafts time . . .
Not my day.
Bye, I gotta run!

Arts and crafts time
at wood shop—
this will sure be fun.
I'll make a birdhouse to protect
Polly from the sun.
With a saw, saw here
and a drill, drill there;
here a bang, there a bang—
this thing will not hang hang.
Arts and crafts time . . .
Not my day.
Bye, I gotta run!

Arts and crafts time:
Moving on . . .
Look—I made a lamp.
I plugged it in and promptly blew
all the lights in camp!
Stitched a moccasin—
foot did not fit in.
Sewed a shirt
(two-sleeved skirt)—
so I'm not an expert.
I'll keep trying arts and crafts
till I'm good at one!

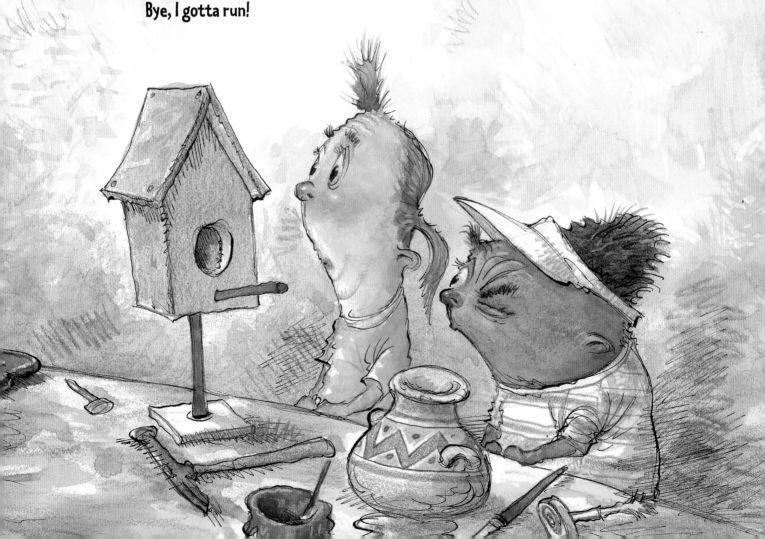

It's Time for Water Sports
(To the tune of "Itsy Bitsy Spider")

I'm jumping in, excited
it's time for water sports.
But, oh no! Disaster—
Mom sent some too-big shorts!
Instructor blows the whistle.
He yells at me and then
I'm ready for some action—
my shorts are on again.

Surfing, sailing, swimming,
a chance to water-ski,
tubing, bodyboarding—
that is the stuff for me.
It's so great to snorkel.
I hear canoeing's cool.
Forget that stuff at this camp,
there's just a wading pool.

4¼ INCHES

L·I·M·B·O
(To the tune of "B·I·N·G·O")

There is a contest—
real big prize—
I'm gonna win at limbo,
L·I·M·B·O.
How low can I go?
Lower than my toe,
'cause I'm real good at limbo!

I'm bending back;
I'm squatting down.
No one beats me at limbo,
L·I·M·B·O.
I am creeping slow,
hardly moving, though
that's how you win at limbo!

It's down to two:
The other kid
is also good at limbo,
L·I·M·B·O.
Thought I was a pro.
She went far below.
What time do we play bingo?

At the Campfire
(To the tune of "Rock-a-Bye Baby")

At the campfire,
hot dog on stick
over the flame—
it cooks up so quick.
When the stick breaks,
the hot dog falls in.
So I just eat mustard.
No wonder I'm thin!

At the campfire,
marshmallows toast.
Stories are told
about the camp ghost.
Kids quake with fear.
How eerie it's been.
No one will sleep all night
in our whole cabin!

At the campfire,
counselor sings,
strumming guitar
on all the wrong strings.
Campfire roars,
and we would all grin
if he'd stop playing
and throw it in!

Jim Needs a Shower
(To the tune of "Pop Goes the Weasel")

My friend Jimmy is a nice kid.
He tells jokes by the hour.
But one fact just cannot be hid:
Jim needs a shower!

He runs, he jumps, he hops, he flips.
In baseball, he's got power.
Water time is what he skips.
Jim needs a shower!

My friend Jimmy oughta get wet.
His body he should scour.
Has he splished or splashed? No, not yet!
Jim needs a shower!

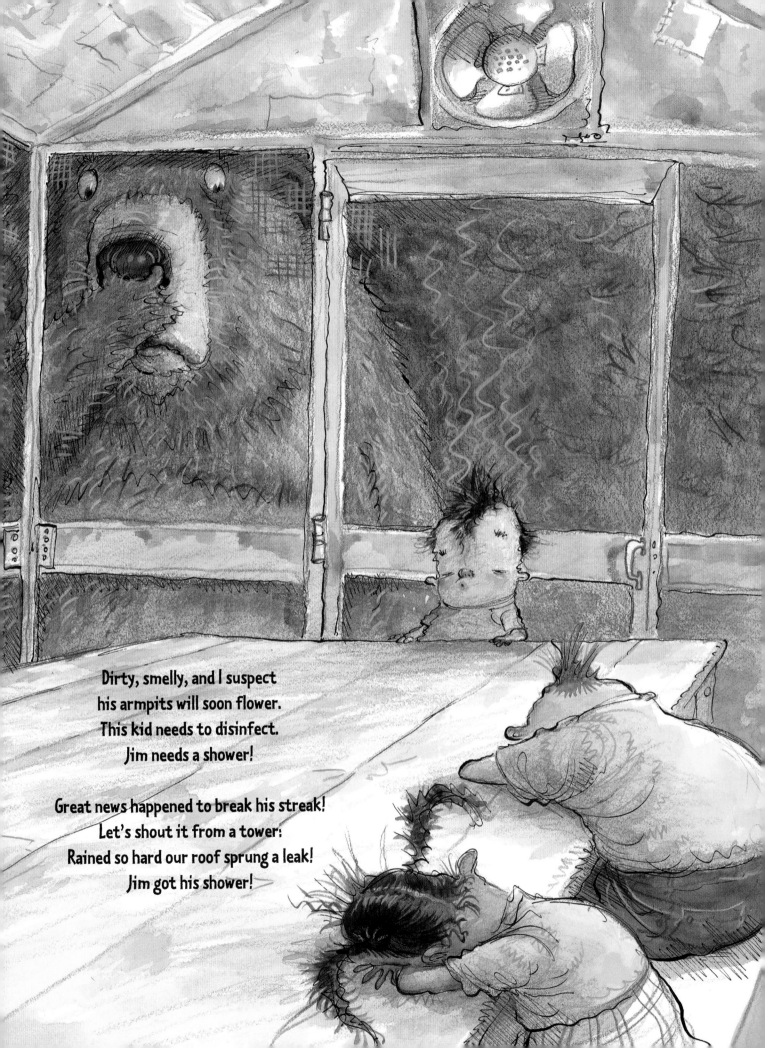

Dirty, smelly, and I suspect
his armpits will soon flower.
This kid needs to disinfect.
Jim needs a shower!

Great news happened to break his streak!
Let's shout it from a tower:
Rained so hard our roof sprung a leak!
Jim got his shower!

Whose Idea Was This Dumb Hike?
(To the tune of "Twinkle, Twinkle Little Star")

Whose idea was this dumb hike?
I would rather ride a bike.
I don't do
well in mud;
lost a shoe
in that crud.
If we get back from this hike,
I am gonna go on strike!

Whose idea was it to climb
up a mountain? Frankly, I'm
not so good
at this height.
Do you think
my name's Kite?
From now on, I will be found
with my feet on solid ground.

Whose idea was camping out?
Roughing it is hard. I doubt
we'll survive
without floors.
I prefer
life indoors.
Such fresh air I do not need.
I'm a city kid, indeed.

This Note's Overdue
(To the tune of "Do Your Ears Hang Low?")

This note's overdue;
it's to ask hey, how are you?
Have you had a lot of fun?
How's baby sister?
What is new?
Well, is Grandma's health improved yet?
And please tell me if you've moved yet.
This note's overdue!

This note's overdue;
it's to answer twelve from you.
And you thought I'd never write,
so this is a dream come true.
Now the family'll proclaim it
quite a miracle and frame it.
This note's overdue!

This note's overdue,
and it comes out of the blue,
but I said that I would write.
I'm a kid who follows through.
I'll stop now; my hand is cramping.
But good news—this won't need stamping.
I'll hand it to you!